Heather Robbins lived on the Canada prairies for most of her adult life, and like many parents, spent her winters taking her son to and from hockey practices and games. The early, frozen mornings, driving to small town hockey rinks were made bearable by seeing the enthusiasm and love of the game in her young son. Her son's experiences in playing in all those games inspired Heather to write a little story, highlighting the activities in the dressing room, as well as on the ice, and touching on the love and support of hockey parents.

Heather now enjoys watching her grandchildren play minor hockey, and again is able to experience the love of the game through the eyes of children.

THE HOCKEY GAME

_____Heather Robbins

AUSTIN MACAULEY PUBLISHERS™
LONDON • CAMBRIDGE • NEW YORK • SHARJAH

Copyright © Heather Robbins (2019)

Ordering Information:
Quantity sales: special discounts are available on quantity purchases by corporations, associations, and others. For details, contact the publisher at the address below.

Robbins, Heather
The Hockey Game

ISBN 9781641826419 (Paperback)
ISBN 9781641826426 (Hardback)
ISBN 9781641826433 (E-Book)

The main category of the book — JUVENILE FICTION / Sports & Recreation / Hockey

www.austinmacauley.com/us

First Published (2019)
Austin Macauley Publishers LLC
40 Wall Street, 28th Floor
New York, NY 10005
USA

mail-usa@austinmacauley.com
+1 (646) 5125767

To all hockey parents and players.

On Saturday morning, I jump out of bed,
With thoughts of the hockey game stuck in my head.

I grab all my gear and race down the stairs,
Run through the kitchen, and leap over the chairs.

"Sit down and eat," my mom says at the sink.
"I can't. There's no time. I must get to the rink!"

My bag feels so heavy as I run down the lane
But all I can think of is today's hockey game.

Into the dressing room, I meet up with my team.
Playing with these guys has been like a dream.

"OK," says the coach. "This is the championship game.
If we win today, well just think of the fame!"

Quickly, we dress and head out to the ice.
We're eager to go so don't tell us twice.

The visiting team looks so fast and so tall.
I feel a bit nervous and skate into the wall!

"Tweet," goes the whistle, the Ref yells, "Let's go!"
We take our positions, at center is Joe.

The puck is then dropped, and Joe passes to me.
I take three or four strides and then pass up to Lee.

The Ref blows the whistle and spreads his arms wide.
The play is now stopped because we are offside.

We face off again, this time they get the puck
And on down the ice, they go fast like a truck.

They pass back and forth and to our goalie, they roar.

Then one takes the shot and...Oh no, they score!!

The rest of the period, we kept them at one.
But I'm sorry to say that they kept us at none!

The second period starts, and we must get a goal.
If they score again we will be in a hole.

Joe gets the puck and he swerves and he dips.
He just about gets to the net when he trips.

"Tweet," goes the whistle, a penalty called.
"Hey, that's not fair!" the other coach bawled.

03:12

Now they're shorthanded, so this is our chance
To tie up this game or get kicked in the pants.

But two minutes go by and we can't get a break.
The second period ends, it's about all I can take!

Our coach soon comes in to give us a talk.
I'm feeling so tired my stick feels like a rock.

I should have listened to mom when she told me to eat.
Then maybe, I wouldn't be so dead on my feet.

Back out on the ice, my energy is gone.
I look up and see my mom cheering me on.

I realize she loves me whether I win or lose.
She says, "Just do your best in all that you choose."

The third period begins and I'm feeling brand new.
The puck comes to me and I fire on cue.

My slap shot is awesome, I just use one stroke.
But too soon I realize my hockey stick broke!

I race for a new one, there's no time to waste.
But now, oh no... my right skate came unlaced.

"Never mind," I say and get back in the game.
I know you would do exactly the same.

With minutes to go, we skate in like a jet,
And finally, yes finally, the puck goes into the net!

Now we are tied with one minute to play.
Who's going to win it? Well, we just may.

"Let's see your slap shot," the coach says to me.

The pressure is on and I have to go pee!

Joe takes the face off, the puck shoots to Rick.
He passes to me and it lands on my stick.

I wind up like a spring and get ready to shoot.
The crowd gets excited, and they howl and hoot.

"Crack," goes my stick as it contacts the puck.
"Swoosh," into the net, can you believe my luck!

The buzzer then goes, the game's over and done.
We all played our best and we had lots of fun.

We shake hands with each other and skate off the ice.
That team we just played is really quite nice.

We each get a medal that sits proud on our chest.
The season is over, and it's just been the best.

On our way home, mom and I walk up the lane.
We smile as we talk about the great hockey game.